What any author wants is for his books to become dog-eared and familiar. I've been lucky enough that my very young readers are particularly adept at giving their books doggy ears in no time at all.

And of all my books, perhaps it's those about Kipper that get the doggiest ears of all, which I guess is kind of appropriate.

Mick Inkpen

More books about Kipper

Kipper
Kipper's Toybox
Kipper's Snowy Day
Kipper's Christmas Eve
Kipper's A to Z
Kipper's New Pet
Kipper's Monster
Kipper's Beach Ball
One Year with Kipper
Hide Me, Kipper
Kipper Story Collection
Kipper's Birthday and
Other Stories

First published in 1993
by Hodder Children's Books

This edition published in 2014

Text and illustrations copyright © Mick Inkpen 1993

Hodder Children's Books
338 Euston Road
London NW1 3BH

Hodder Children's Books Australia
Level 17/207 Kent Street
Sydney, NSW 2000

ISBN: 978 1 444 91817 5
10 9 8 7 6 5 4 3 2 1

Printed in China

Hodder Children's Books is a division of
Hachette Children's Books.
An Hachette UK Company.
www.hachette.co.uk

Kipper's Birthday

Mick Inkpen

Hodder
Children's
Books

A division of Hachette Children's Books

It was the day before Kipper's birthday. He was busy with his paints making party invitations. In large letters he painted,

Plees come to my bithday party tomoro at 12 o cloc dont be lat

He hung them up to dry and set about making a cake.

Kipper had not made a cake before. He put some currants and eggs and currants and flour and sugar and currants into a bowl. Then he stirred the mixture until his arm ached.

Next he added some cherries and stirred it once more. Then he rolled it with a rolling pin and looked at what he had made.

'I have made a flat thing,'
he said.

Kipper squeezed the flat thing into a cake shape and watched it bake in the oven. To his surprise it changed itself slowly into a sort of heap, but it smelled good. He put the last remaining cherry on the top for decoration.

By this time the party invitations were dry.

'I'll deliver them tomorrow,' yawned Kipper. 'It's too late now.'

Kipper woke bright and early on his birthday. His first thought was, 'Balloons! We must have balloons!' But as he rushed downstairs another thought popped into his head. 'Invitations!'

Kipper ran all the way to his best friend's house and stuffed the invitations into Tiger's hand.

'That one's yours! Those are for the others!' he panted. 'Can't stop! Balloons!'

When he had gone Tiger opened the invitation.

Plees come to my bithday party tomoro at 12 o cloc dont be lat

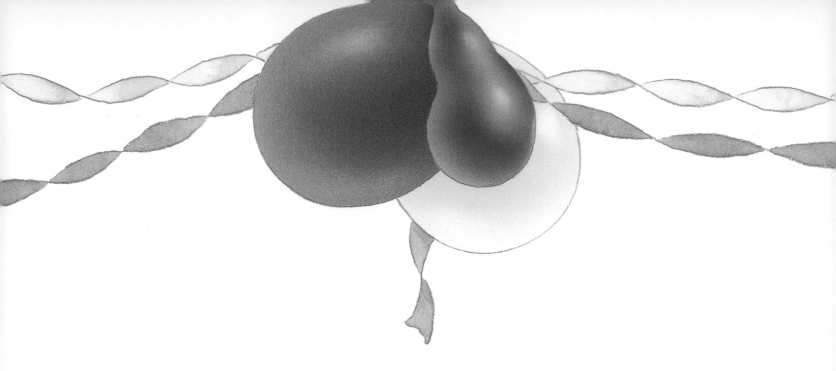

At twelve o'clock Kipper carefully placed his cake on the table and sat down to wait for a knock at the door.

He waited. And he waited. But nobody came. Not even Tiger.

The cake smelled good and Kipper began to feel hungry. At one o'clock he ate the cherry from the top.

Two o'clock passed. Still nobody came. Kipper pulled off a large piece of cake and broke it open to see if there was a cherry inside. There were two. He ate them both and began to feel better.

By five o'clock there were no more cherries to be found.

Kipper stretched out on the table feeling very full and very sleepy.

Kipper slept through the evening and into the night. He dreamt that he was climbing a mountain made of cake and dodging great cake boulders as they crashed towards him.

Even when the sun streamed through his window the next morning he did not wake, but snored peacefully until noon when he was woken by a knock at the door.

His friends had come. 'Happy birthday, Kipper!' said Jake.

'Happy birthday, Kipper!' said Holly.

'And many happy returns!' said Tiger.

Kipper blinked and rubbed his eyes.

'But my birthday was yesterday,' he said sleepily.

They looked at the invitation.

Plees come to my bithday party tomoro at 12 o cloc dont be lat

Kipper looked puzzled.
'So my birthday is not until tomorrow,' he said. 'We haven't missed it after all!'

'No, no, no,' said Tiger.
'Your birthday must have been
tomorrow the day before yesterday.'
Kipper looked puzzled again.

Tiger went on, 'So yesterday it
would have been *today*, but today
it was *yesterday*. Do you see?'

Kipper did not see.
His brain was beginning
to ache so he said,
'Cake anyone?'
And then he
remembered that
he had eaten
it all.

'Never mind,' said Tiger. 'Why don't you open your presents?'

The presents seemed a bit odd.

The first was a napkin from Jake.

The second was some candles from Holly.

'Very useful,' said Kipper, trying not to look disappointed.

But the third was the most useful of all…

It was a cake!

'My children absolutely LOVE all of Mick Inkpen's books, and I still love reading Kipper to them, even when it's for the hundredth time. . .'

CRESSIDA COWELL

'He is the perfect pup to grow up with. . .'

HILARY MCKAY

'Storytelling at its best.' DAVID MELLING